KING KONG

Anthony Browne's
KING KONG

FROM THE STORY CONCEIVED BY
EDGAR WALLACE & MERIAN C. COOPER

PICTURE CORGI

In memory of my dad; for me,
the original Kong.
A.B.

KING KONG
A PICTURE CORGI BOOK 978 0 552 55384 1

First published in Great Britain by Julia MacRae,
an imprint of Random House Children's Publishers UK

Julia MacRae edition published 1994
Picture Corgi edition published 2005

13

Picture Corgi Books are published by Random House Children's Publishers UK,
61-63 Uxbridge Road, London W5 5SA,
a division of The Random House Group Ltd,
Addresses for companies within The Random House Group Limited
can be found at: www.randomhouse.co.uk/offices.htm

THE RANDOM HOUSE GROUP Limited Reg. No. 954009
www.randomhousechildrens.co.uk

A CIP catalogue record for this book is available from the British Library.

Printed in China

What the Beast said was quite good sense, though it was not what one might call intelligent conversation. But every day Beauty observed some new kindness in him, and as she became used to seeing him, she also became accustomed to his ugliness.

BEAUTY AND THE BEAST

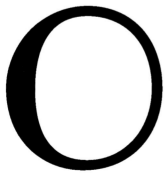NCE UPON A TIME IN NEW YORK CITY the evening sky was growing dark and a thin veil of snow was falling. The streets were crowded; old men with shopping bags, couples out on dates, people going home from work. The city was a never-ending tide of human beings.

One person seemed to be swimming against that tide. He was Carl Denham, a film director, known as the craziest man in Hollywood. Denham always made his films in distant, dangerous places and rumours were spreading throughout the film world about his next film – it was to be his most ambitious yet.

Denham was about to go on location. He had a ship waiting at the New Jersey docks, due to sail at six the next morning. In fact, if the ship *didn't* sail, there would be trouble. The authorities had heard that guns and gas bombs were on board, so the ship would be searched.

But Denham didn't have the one thing he needed to make his film. It was going to be the best picture he'd ever made, but it needed a young, beautiful woman. He'd tried every acting agency in New York, and they had all turned him down. "You take too many risks," they said, "and you won't even tell us where you're going. No actress will take that job."

That was why Denham was walking the streets of New York, looking for the right face for his film, the face of Beauty. He looked into thousands of faces; faces in shops, faces on park benches, faces in cafés, faces in queues. Sad faces, happy faces. But not one of them was the right face, *the* face, for his greatest ever film.

Denham was tired, and there wasn't much time left. He stopped at a store to get something to eat. That was when he saw the hand. It was a very beautiful hand . . . and it was about to steal an apple.

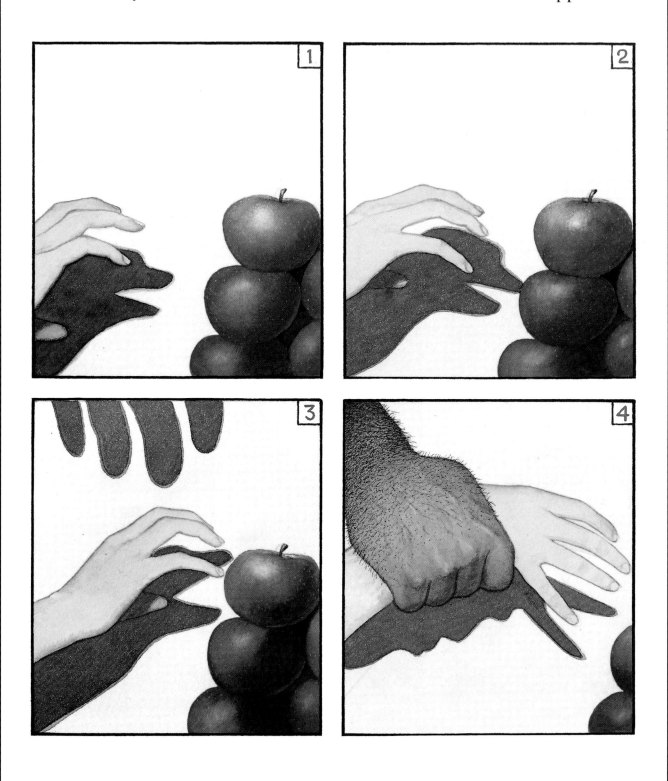

"Gotcha!" screamed the shopkeeper. "You little thief! I'm callin' the cops!"

"No!" cried the woman. "I didn't take it. Let me go."

"That's true," Denham butted in. "She didn't touch the apples." He gave the shopkeeper a dollar. "Here, take this, and shut up!"

The woman looked up at Denham. "Thanks," she said.

It was only then that Denham saw her face. He was astounded – it was the face he had been searching for!

It was the face of Beauty.

Half an hour later Denham and the woman were sitting in a café. She had just finished her first proper meal for weeks. She told him that her name was Ann Darrow, she was down on her luck with no money and no job. Denham couldn't stop looking at her. She was a film director's dream – he'd never seen anyone so beautiful.

"Ever done any acting?" he asked.

"I've been an extra over on Long Island a few times. The studio's closed down now."

"I'm Carl Denham," he explained. "Ever heard of me?"

"Y-yes," said Ann. "You make moving pictures. In jungles and places."

"That's me. And *you're* going to star in my next picture. We sail at six!"

Ann gaped at him.

"Don't just sit there, Ann," Denham said. "Come on! We've got to buy you some new clothes and get you to the hairdresser."

The next morning Ann Darrow slowly opened her eyes. What was different?

It was the first morning for a very long time that she had woken up without feeling hungry. Ann saw a bowl of apples next to her bed and remembered what had happened. She was in a cabin, on a ship called the *Wanderer*. Her room was gently rocking up and down, and the engines hummed under her feet – so they were already on their way.

Then she saw all the boxes – dress boxes, hat boxes and shoe boxes. To someone as poor as Ann they were the most magical sight in the world.

Ann spent over an hour getting ready. She couldn't believe her luck; yesterday she had been dressed in rags, and so hungry that she'd been ready to steal – today she was dressed like a princess, fed like a queen, *and* she had a job! There was just the slight nagging worry that Denham hadn't said where they were going, but Ann convinced herself that she could trust him . . . more or less.

She left the cabin and set out to explore the ship. A man was shouting orders at the crew. He was the first mate, Jack Driscoll, and he didn't notice her as one of the sailors dropped a rope. "Don't put it there!" Driscoll yelled. "It goes over here." He swung back his arm and hit Ann in the face.

"What are *you* doing up here?" he asked gruffly.

"I-I just wanted to see . . ."

"Oh, you must be that girl Denham picked up last night . . . I should warn you, I don't think much of women on ships. Still, I am sorry I hit you. Hope it didn't hurt."

"Oh, it's okay," said Ann. "I'm sort of used to it."

For Ann the days just glided by; she loved life aboard the *Wanderer*. The rest, fresh air and good food made her feel like a new woman. Work on the film was going well, she spent hours each day in front of Denham's camera. The director tested her face from every possible angle and found her perfect. Ann was a little concerned that he kept asking her to scream as though she'd seen something terrible, but she was having so much fun that she pushed this disturbing thought to the back of her mind.

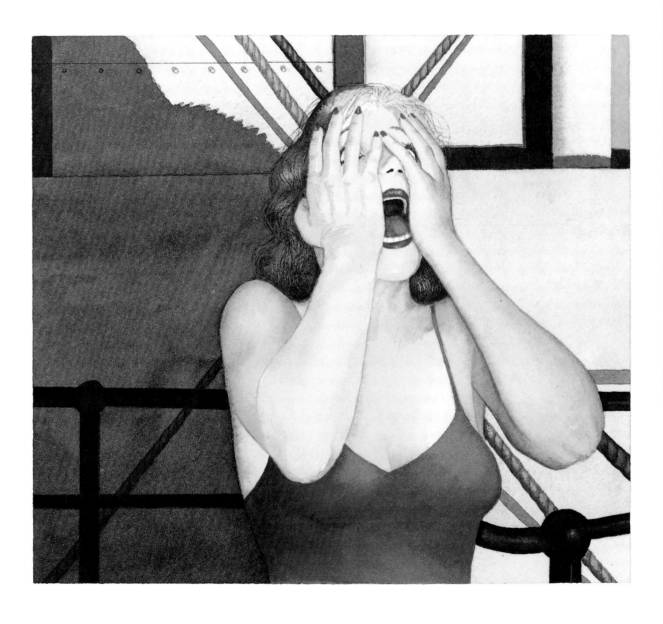

Ann and Jack gradually became very close friends. Jack wasn't used to women but he found Ann easy to talk to. As they got to know and like each other, Jack started to worry about what would happen to her when they reached their destination. The ship had already sailed through the Panama Canal, past Hawaii, Japan, the Philippines and Sumatra, and still Denham hadn't told them where they were going. Jack decided it was time to find out, so he went to confront Denham.

"Hey, Denham!" Jack said. "You've got to let us know what's happening. Where are we heading? What crazy plans have you got this time?"

Denham raised an eyebrow. "What's this, Jack? You going soft on me?"

"'Course I'm not," Driscoll said. "It's Ann . . ."

"Oh!" said Denham. "You've gone soft on *her*." He frowned. "As if I haven't got enough problems without you falling in love."

"Who said anything about . . ?" Jack blushed.

"I always thought you were a real tough guy, Jack," Denham went on. "But if Beauty gets you . . ." He laughed. "It's just like my movie. The Beast is a tough guy, tougher than anyone – he can lick the world. But when he sees Beauty, she gets him. Think about it, Jack."

Driscoll stared angrily at Denham and the director laughed. "Come on, Jack. Let's go see the skipper. It's time I gave you both some answers."

They found Captain Engelhorn in the chart room looking at a map.

"We're *here*, Denham," he said, pointing. "You promised some facts when we got to this spot, so tell me where we're going."

"Southwest," snapped Denham.

"Southwest?" said Engelhorn. "But – there's nothing there!"

"Nothing but *this!*" said Denham. He took a piece of paper out of his pocket. "I got this map from an old Norwegian sea captain. He's a man I trust, not the sort to make up tales, so I know this is real."

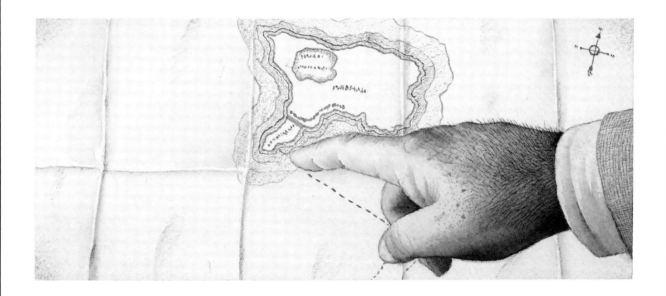

"That wall," said Denham, "is higher than twenty men, and hundreds of years old. The natives of the island don't know when the wall was built, or who built it – but they keep it strong, just the same."

"Why?" asked Jack.

"Because there's something on the other side," answered Denham. "Something they fear." He lowered his voice. "Have either of you ever heard of . . . Kong?"

"Why . . . yes," Engelhorn replied uneasily. "The Malay people talk about him. Some kind of god or devil, isn't he?"

"A monster," said Denham. "He holds the island in a grip of fear. I'm going to find that beast and put him in my picture!"

Jack gulped. The Beast . . . Denham's movie was going to be about Beauty and the Beast! The image of Ann Darrow's face came into his mind and Jack Driscoll was suddenly afraid.

A few days later the ship was wrapped in a blanket of fog, and slowed down to a crawl. Denham, Driscoll and Ann were on deck with the captain, impatiently waiting for their first glimpse of the island. From down below came the voice of a sailor measuring the depth of the water. "Thirty fathoms!" he called. "Twenty-five fathoms! Twenty fathoms! Ten!"

"We're closing in fast," said Engelhorn. "Driscoll, tell them to drop anchor."

Jack gave the order, and they heard the anchor splash into the ocean. At the same moment they heard another, chilling sound.

"Drums!" said Driscoll.

As they listened, a wind came up and the fog parted like a curtain. There, right in front of them, was the island, less than a quarter of a mile away.

"Skull Mountain!" shouted Denham. "D'you see it? And the wall! Look at that wall!" His eyes were wild with excitement.

"Get out the boats!" he screamed. "Everyone to the island!"

They were on the beach in less than an hour, and came to a village that at first seemed deserted, but the ominous drumming got louder and louder.

"They must be having some sort of ceremony!" said Denham, barely concealing his excitement. Suddenly a wailing chant of "Kong! Kong!" rose above the drums.

"Listen!" said Denham. "They're calling for Kong. You all stay here. I'll go on ahead and see what's happening."

He was back in a flash. "Everyone keep quiet," he whispered. "Get the cameras rolling! Follow me!"

They crept forward and came to a great square packed with natives dancing and chanting, "Kong! Kong!" At the far end of the square was the massive wall. Stone steps led up to a huge gate, in front of which knelt a beautiful girl wearing a necklace of flowers. Denham had his cameras running – this was even better than he had hoped for. What a film this would be!

Suddenly the drumbeats changed and a group of men dressed as apes leaped up on to the steps. The weird chanting was louder than ever: "Kong! Kong! Kong!" Now it was the chief's turn to enter the dance. He stood up, but he never began his part, for at that moment he saw the strangers. *"Bado!"* he screeched. *"Bado! Dama pati vego!"*

The drums stopped, the chanting stopped. Everyone stood still. There was dead silence.

"Easy, boys," said Denham quietly. "Remember, we're the ones with the guns. Don't make any sudden moves."

The chief lifted his hand and all the tribesmen raised their spears.

"Watu!" shouted the chief. *"Tama di? Tama di?"*

"That's lucky," said Captain Engelhorn. "I can speak their language." He stepped forward. "Greetings!" he called. "We are your friends. *Bala! Bala!* Friends!"

"Tasko! Tasko!" the chief yelled.

"That means get out," said Engelhorn.

"Talk him out of it," ordered Denham. "Ask him what the funny dance is all about."

Engelhorn spoke to the chief and pointed to the kneeling girl. The chief's answer didn't seem to please the captain.

"He says she's going to be the bride of Kong."

Jack quickly moved in front of Ann but it was too late, the witch doctor had already seen her. *"Malem!"* he screamed. *"Malem me pakeno! Kow bisa para Kong!"*

"The woman of gold!" said Engelhorn. "That witch doctor wants Ann. He's probably never seen anyone with blonde hair before, says he'll trade six of his women for her."

"Tell him it's no deal," said Denham.

The captain and the chief continued their strange conversation. "I told him we'd talk again tomorrow," said Captain Engelhorn.

"Right, let's get back to the ship," Denham ordered. "We'll go slowly, with big smiles on our faces. You men there – you go first. Keep Ann in the middle, and keep your guns ready."

They were soon back in the boat, heading quickly for the ship. Ann was the first to speak. "Wow! I don't know about all of you, but I wouldn't have missed that for the world!"

As the sun went down, Ann looked over the water and listened to the sinister beating of the drums. Jack joined her.

"Why aren't you in bed?" he asked.

"I couldn't sleep. The sound of those drums makes me nervous, I guess."

"Me, too," said Jack. "Denham was crazy letting you go ashore today. I dread to think what he'll want you to do for this picture."

"After what he's done for me," Ann said, "I'd take just about any risk for him."

"Don't say that, Ann. When I think of what might have happened today . . . if anything *had* happened to you . . ."

"Well, then," Ann smiled. "You wouldn't have been bothered by having a woman on board."

"Please Ann, don't laugh, you know I'm scared for you. You know . . . I love you."

As she kissed him, they heard Captain Engelhorn calling Jack to the bridge, but when he left her neither of them heard the gentle splash of oars in the water.

Ann yawned, and looked around the deck; there was no-one about. Suddenly a huge hand clamped over her mouth and powerful arms grabbed her from behind! She twisted and turned and struggled but it was no use. She was lifted helplessly over the ship's rail, where more strong hands grasped her and pulled her down into the bottom of a canoe. The hand was still pressed tightly over her mouth so she couldn't make a sound. She could feel the canoe heading swiftly for the shore. Ann was terrified.

When they reached land, Ann was lifted into the air and carried to the great square. Again it was packed with people, chanting and dancing in the torchlight. The drums beat relentlessly. Ann saw a face she recognised; it was the girl who had been kneeling on the steps that afternoon. Ann shuddered when she realised what was different about her now – she was dressed like all the other women. Ann was carried up the steps and a necklace of flowers was placed over her head. Six terrifying men dressed as gorillas began to dance wildly around her.

The awful truth was now clear – she had taken the girl's place. *She* was to be the new bride of Kong!

On the *Wanderer*, just before midnight, Lumpy, the ship's cook, found a wooden bracelet on the deck. "On deck!" he shouted. "All hands on deck!" The men hurried up from below.

"Look!" Lumpy yelled. "Those savages have been here!"

A quick search of the ship confirmed what they feared – Ann was missing.

"To the boat!" shouted Denham. "I want a rifle for every man, and don't forget the bombs!" The sailors leapt into the boat, and raced for shore.

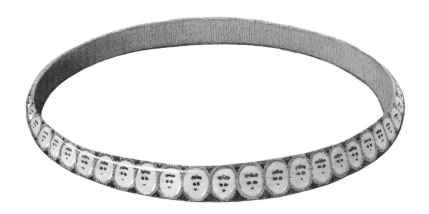

Ann saw the massive gates slowly opening in front of her as she was lifted up and taken through. The natives carried her to a high stone altar at the edge of the jungle, and tied her wrists to two columns. The men hurried back to the village, the gates closed, and a huge wooden bolt was pushed into place. A deafening metal gong sounded, and the chanting and drumming stopped. The whole tribe gathered along the top of the wall, their torches lighting the sky. Once again they began their chant: "Kong! Kong! Kong! Kong!"

Ann was frantic with fear. She wrestled with the ropes on her wrists like an animal caught in a trap, she screamed and begged, but it was no use. The chanting got louder and louder: "Kong! Kong! Kong! KONG!"

Then suddenly the chanting stopped again, and she felt an unbearable silence. Very slowly a huge black shadow fell over her.

A terrible, terrible roar filled the night air, and a hideous beast came crashing out of the jungle. It was Kong!

The monster stood up on his toes, pounded his chest and roared angrily at the people on the wall. Then he saw Ann, and his roaring stopped.

The natives waited, holding their breath, hoping that Kong would accept the woman of gold. He carefully freed her wrists, and picked her up with great gentleness. There was a loud crack and a bullet whistled past Kong's ear, but he didn't notice. It seemed his only thought was of his new treasure, so he didn't see the gate open or the men who slipped through. Kong gave another mighty roar, turned, and carried Ann into the jungle.

Jack Driscoll had fired the gun; he appeared to be the leader now. "I'm going in to get Ann back!" he said. "I'll need a dozen men. Who's coming with me?" He and Denham chose ten of the men, and left Engelhorn in charge of those staying behind in the village.

The search party set out past the altar, following Kong's path of destruction through the jungle. "Hey, look at this!" yelled one of the men a while later. "Look at this incredible footprint!" Each man shivered.

They found more prints and followed them. It was hard climbing through the thick, dark jungle and difficult to see anything. At last they heard the welcome sound of birds singing. Daylight was coming.

The sun rose and they found themselves in a clearing. In the undergrowth ahead of them something moved. One of the men gave a startled cry of fear, and an enormous creature came crashing out of the jungle straight towards them.

"Quick!" shouted Jack. "The bombs! When I throw, everyone hit the ground!"

As the monster got closer and closer, Jack hurled a bomb straight at it. There was an ear-splitting explosion. The men dived for cover and still they heard the footsteps getting nearer, nearer . . . but slower. Then the footsteps stopped. The ground shook as the gigantic creature fell.

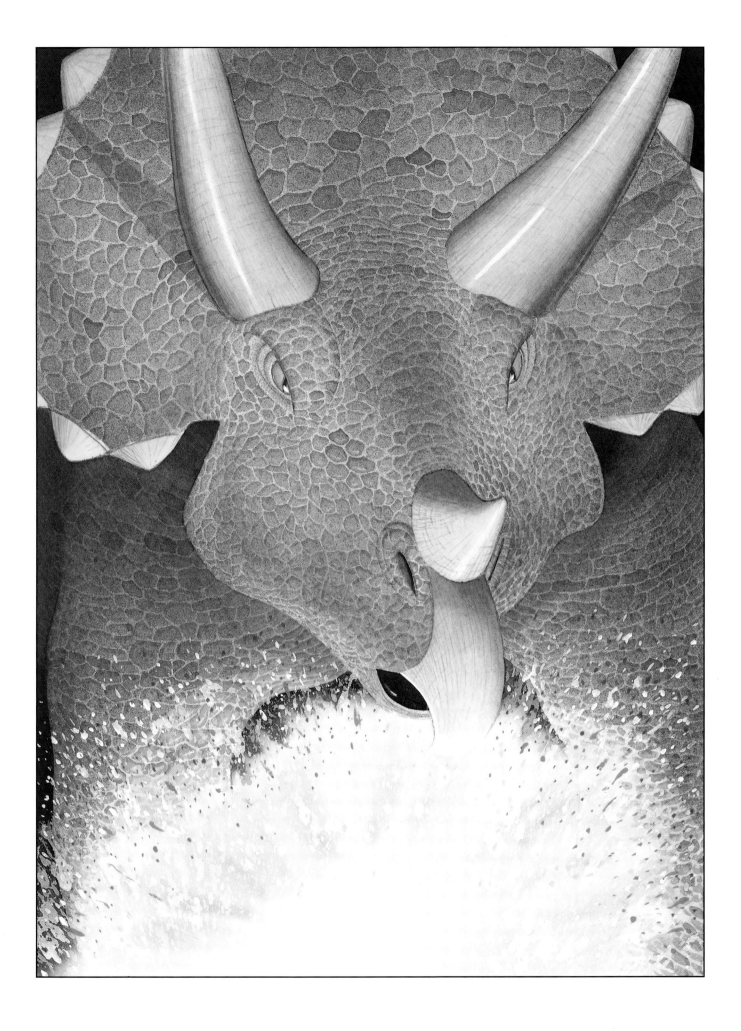

When they felt sure it really was dead, the men crowded round for a closer look. "It's a dinosaur!" said Denham. "These things have been extinct for millions of years."

"Not on Skull Mountain Island," Jack replied. "Kong must be some kind of prehistoric animal too. This place could be swarming with monsters!"

They picked up Kong's tracks again where the trail began to slope down, leading into a valley wreathed in fog. Before them was a small lake. The men stopped at the water's edge as they heard loud splashing ahead. "Kong's swimming across," said Jack. "We can't do that with these bombs and guns. We'll have to build a raft."

The sailors worked quickly, cutting down trees and tying them together with vines. When they had finished, there was barely enough room for them all on board, and the raft lurched perilously from one side to the other, but they managed to get most of the way across. Then the raft shook as it hit something just below the surface. The 'thing' moved.

"Dinosaur!" cried Denham.

A huge head rose out of the lake, and the raft was tossed high in the air. The men were thrown into the water and struggled frantically towards the shore. Jack Driscoll got there first, and as he turned round he saw the dinosaur coming after them. The men caught up with him and they all tried to run through the swamp towards the jungle.

On and on they battled, hearing the monster closer and closer behind them, but eventually they reached the safety of the dense undergrowth. All except one man. They heard a horrifying scream, shuddered, then plunged deeper into the jungle.

Soon they came to a deep chasm. The only way to get to the other side was over a log bridging the gap. Jack Driscoll climbed on to the log, and the others followed. Driscoll had just crossed when they all heard a terrible roar. In front of them was Kong!

Jack grabbed a vine and climbed down the ravine, where he hid in a shallow cave. Denham, who was last, managed to scramble back to the other side. The rest were trapped, as Kong lifted the log and swung it back and forth. The terrified men desperately tried to hold on as long as they could, but one by one they fell screaming to their deaths.

Kong reached a great hairy hand into the cave where Jack was hiding. Jack slashed a finger with his knife and Kong howled with anger. Immediately there was a loud answering scream. "Help! He-e-e-l-p!" It was Ann.

An Allosaurus was coming towards her. Kong forgot about Driscoll and rushed back to save Ann. The dinosaur was even bigger than Kong, with long, sharp teeth and powerful hind legs, but Kong was a clever fighter. Again and again he tricked the other beast into moving, then darted in with vicious blows or bites. Kong leapt on to the creature's back, pinned the dinosaur down, and tore apart its jaws.

In triumph Kong threw back his head, roared, and beat his chest. Then he carefully picked Ann up, and set off deeper into the jungle.

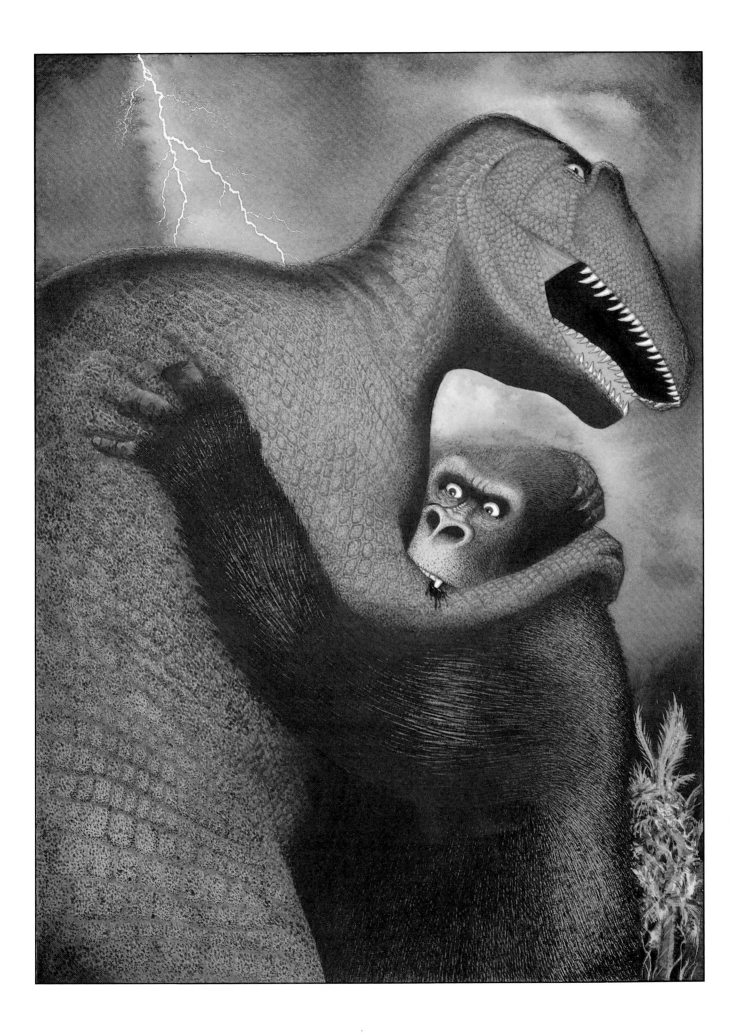

Jack Driscoll and Carl Denham faced each other across the chasm.

"You go back!" shouted Jack. "Get some more men, and more bombs! I'll follow Kong, and when I find him I'll signal to you somehow."

"Okay, Jack! Be careful . . . and good luck!" Denham turned and ran back towards the village.

Following Kong's trail was hard work and Jack was hungry and tired, but the giant beast seemed to go faster with every step. Jack realised that they were climbing up the back of Skull Mountain.

He's heading for home, thought Jack. It made sense; Kong was the only animal on the island who could climb, so up here he was safe.

Jack climbed wearily on, and finally as he neared the top he saw Kong entering a huge cave. So *this* was his home!

Jack crawled into the cave and saw Kong put Ann on a high ledge. Kong turned his back on her, and Jack watched in horror as a giant snake slithered out of a steaming pool and lunged towards her. Ann screamed, Kong turned and leaped on to the reptile. The snake coiled itself round Kong's neck, and seemed to be squeezing the life out of the giant ape. He fought furiously to free himself, and with one last effort managed to dash the snake against the rocks, breaking its neck.

Kong picked up Ann again and made his way to an opening near the roof of the cave, closely followed by Jack.

The beast emerged on to a ledge overlooking the island, gently put Ann down and roared his defiance at the world. He sat down, carefully lifted Ann up, and examined her properly for the first time. He seemed fascinated.

From his hiding place Jack dislodged a boulder and Kong rushed to see what it was. Jack cowered back, sure the beast was about to discover him, when suddenly there was a loud beating of wings. A great flying reptile swooped down on Ann and grasped her in its claws. Kong was only just in time to seize the huge creature as it lifted Ann into the air. Again Kong had to fight for his life to save his bride, and a bloody battle began as the reptile dropped Ann.

It was the chance Jack needed. He ran to Ann's side.

"Ann," he called softly.

"Jack! Oh, I knew you'd come."

They quickly embraced, then Jack leaned over the edge and looked down. Far below them lay a dark pool. Ann saw a long liana hanging from the ledge.

"Quick, Jack! We could climb down that!"

There was no time to think about the danger, so with Ann clinging tightly to him, Jack began the perilous descent.

Kong finally killed the giant reptile and ripped it apart with his teeth. Jack and Ann saw its broken body hurtle past them.

Then Kong looked for his bride. He saw her and roared with anger. Ann and Jack felt themselves being lifted up as Kong seized the liana, and pulled it towards him. Ann could feel Kong's hot breath as they were dragged ever nearer. She was afraid to look up at the beast's awful face, and terrified to look down into the abyss. Finally she could hold on no longer and fell. Jack leaped after her.

Down and down they sank into the dark, silent water. Ann felt she would die before coming up for air, but at last she emerged spluttering into the bright sunlight. She noticed with a thrill how loud the birds sang, then exploded with joy when she saw Jack emerge. They struggled towards each other and hugged tightly as they were swept down the river.

At the native village night was falling, and there was still no signal from Driscoll. Denham was assembling a search party when Jack and Ann were seen by a lookout as they came towards the wall. They were utterly exhausted.

"You're safe now, we'll soon have you back on the ship," said Engelhorn.

"Wait a minute!" said Denham. "What about Kong? We came here to make a movie, but we've got something here worth more than all the movies in the world. And we've got those gas bombs – we could catch him alive!"

"You're crazy!" Jack said. "He's on a cliff where a whole army couldn't get him."

"Yeah, *if* he stays there," said Denham. "But we've got something he wants."

"Something he won't get again," snapped Jack.

"Kong's coming!" shouted the lookout.

"Quick!" yelled Denham. "Close the gates!"

Swiftly the men closed and bolted the gates, just as Kong hurled himself against them. Natives swarmed out of their huts to help hold back the gates, but Kong repeatedly threw himself against them until the bolt shattered and they swung open.

The enraged beast stormed through the village crushing everything in his path. Houses were torn apart, their occupants trampled to death, everything was in chaos. Natives vainly tried hurling spears at the rampaging monster but they merely served to anger him more.

The sailors and film-makers had fled to the boat, but Kong saw them. He was determined to get Ann back, and walked towards the beach. Denham was waiting for him and threw one of the gas bombs.

It exploded in a great flash at Kong's feet. The beast stopped, a look of bewilderment on his face, staggered forward a bit, then fell in slow motion, to land with a deafening thud on the sand.

"Quick, men!" shouted Denham. "We've gotta build a raft and float him to the ship!"

"No chains will hold *that*," said Captain Engelhorn.

"We'll give him more than chains," said Denham. "He's always been king of his world, but we'll teach him fear! You know, the whole world will pay to see this. We're millionaires, boys! In a few months it'll be up in lights: KONG – THE EIGHTH WONDER OF THE WORLD!"

And so the mighty Kong was captured.

Weeks later in New York City excited crowds jammed Times Square. It seemed as though everyone in the city was there, pushing and shoving, frantically trying to get into one theatre.

Soon the theatre was packed tight, and as the lights went down there was an excited air of expectation as Denham came on to the stage.

"Ladies and gentlemen!" he announced. "I'm here tonight to tell you a very strange story, a story so strange no-one will believe it. But, ladies and gentlemen, seeing is believing, and we've brought back the living proof of our adventure. I want you to see for yourselves the greatest thing your eyes have ever beheld. He was a king and a god in the world he knew, but now he comes to civilisation merely a captive, a show to gratify your curiosity.

So, ladies and gentlemen, behold the Eighth Wonder of the World. The mighty – KING KONG!"

The curtain rose, and there was Kong standing in chains on top of a steel platform. The audience gasped, and shifted about uneasily. Nervous laughter slowly spread round the auditorium.

Denham held up a hand. "There is the Beast, ladies and gentle-men. Now I'd like you to meet Beauty – the bravest little girl in the world – Miss Ann Darrow, and her future husband, the man who saved her from the Beast – Mr Jack Driscoll!"

Ann went first on to the stage and Jack followed. The audience cheered wildly. There was a low growl from Kong.

"It's all right, Ann," whispered Denham:"We've knocked some of the fight out of him since you last saw him."

He turned to the audience. "Now folks, you'll have the privilege of seeing the very first photographs taken of Kong and his captors!"

As a group of newspaper photographers came on to the stage, Kong roared with frustration.

"Don't worry, folks," called Denham. "Those chains are made of chrome steel. Jack, put your arm round her, and move closer to Kong, Ann. Let's get Beauty and the Beast in the same picture."

Lights flashed and cameras clicked.

There came a terrible roar from Kong as he strained with all his might against the chains.

With another great roar, Kong broke the chains. The audience
screamed and started to run for the doors. Within seconds Kong was
free. Ann and Jack were carried along in the panic-stricken crowd,
and escaped into the street.

"To my hotel!" cried Jack. "Right over there!"

Kong smashed through the wall of the theatre into the street just in
time to see them enter the hotel.

In his room Jack sat on the bed with Ann, trying to comfort her.

"You're safe now, love," he said.

"It's like some horrible dream," Ann said. "It's like being back on that island again."

"Don't worry, I'll stay here with you . . . anyway, they're bound to get him."

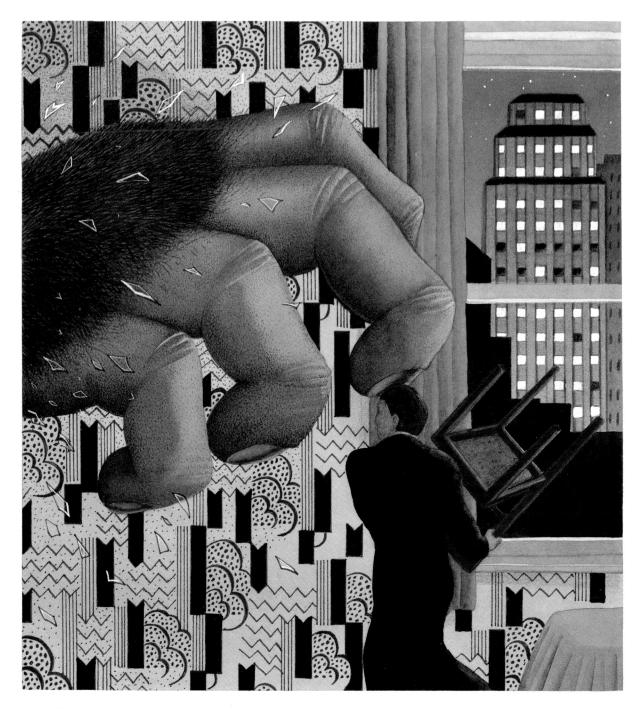

Neither of them saw the massive face at the window. Kong had climbed up the side of the hotel. He smashed his fist through the glass, knocked Jack aside as if he were a baby, pulled the bed towards the window and carefully lifted Ann out. Then he was off into the night, gently cradling his precious woman of gold.

Jack pounded down the stairs and met Denham coming up.

"Kong got Ann!" Jack cried. "We must get help!"

All the sirens in the city seemed to be part of the chase as police cars, fire-engines and ambulances screeched round corners. Above them Kong was travelling fast, scattering terrified crowds in his wake.

"He's headed for Thirty-fourth Street," said Denham.

"The Empire State Building!" Jack cried. "The highest place in the city! That's where he'll go."

By sunrise Kong was halfway up the Empire State Building. Denham and Driscoll were at police headquarters trying to work out a plan with the Police Commissioner.

"We can't get near him," said Denham. "He's still got Ann."

"There's one thing we could try," Jack said. "Aeroplanes! If he puts her down and they can fly close enough to pick him off without hitting her . . ."

Four Navy pursuit craft were dispatched, each carrying powerful machine guns. They approached the Empire State Building just as Kong reached the top. He saw the strange 'birds' and carefully laid Ann on a ledge. Then he stood up straight, beat his great chest and roared his dreadful roar.

The aeroplanes dived towards him, guns blazing. Kong made futile attempts to swat them out of the air as the bullets ripped into his body. One plane flew too near, was grabbed and thrown to the ground. But the others circled again and again. Kong was helpless to stop their fire.

He fought long and bravely but in vain. The planes just kept coming, and at last, weakened by his terrible wounds, Kong stumbled, and seemed to know that he was dying. Ignoring his enemies he picked up Ann and looked at her with great sad eyes, then put her back on the ledge and stroked her tenderly with his fingertips.

Again the planes dived and a final spray of bullets pierced Kong's throat. He was mortally wounded. With a last roar, Kong toppled from the tower.

A moment later Jack arrived at the top of the building and took Ann in his arms. "Ann! Ann, it's all over!"

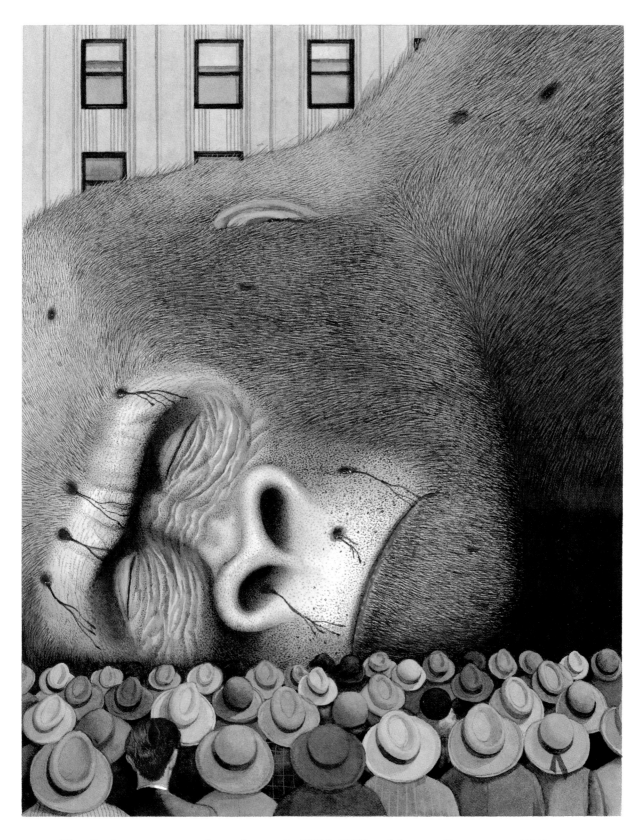

Far below a crowd gathered. "Well!" said a policeman. "That was some fight. But the planes got him in the end."

Denham shook his head ruefully.
"Oh no, it wasn't the aeroplanes . . .
It was *Beauty* that killed the Beast."

Other books by Anthony Browne

My Dad

My Mum

The Night Shimmy

The Shape Game

Voices in the Park

Willy and Hugh

Willy the Wizard

Zoo